THE CONSENT OF SHADOWS

The Consent of Shadows

Written by Naza Semoniff

Published by Semoniff Publishing

CONTENTS

PROLOGUE

Violence has never been the most effective form of control. Nor fear. Nor even the law.

It is a certainty.

A world so painstakingly built, so perfectly maintained, that challenging it is not only dangerous—it is unthinkable.

A man wakes up. The system greets him before his own thoughts form. News reports reassure him that the world is stable. The numbers validate it. The screens confirm it. He does not question.

What good is asking if no one answers?

Questioning isn't just dangerous. It's unthinkable.

The system does not compel him to comply. It offers it. And he chooses it—every single day.

Even deep in the coded architecture of the city, beneath the layers of sanctioned reality, there are fractures. Glitches. Small, near-invisible lapses in the fabric of certainty. A malfunctioning streetlight. Logging the timestamp before the actual occurrence. A name—later gone—from the records.

It fixes them before anyone notices.

But not everyone is blind.

History is not a record of progress. It is a record of control.

Empires have risen and fallen. People have crowned and overthrown kings. Nations built on the promise of freedom have only perfected the instruments of tyranny. The names of the rulers change, but the methods stay the same.

Plato warned of this in The Republic—that those who control the stories, who construct the narrative, hold the true power.

Machiavelli understood it, advising rulers to shape perception rather than waste energy on force.

In Orwell's imagination, a powerful enough entity could demand that two plus two equals five, thus rewriting reality with the stroke of a pen.

Gustave Le Bon dissected the crowd—its weak psychology, its readiness to surrender individuality once submerged in the collective.

An individual voice can resist. A crowd, however, is pliable. Its memory is short. Its passions easily bought. Belief overrides truth.

Where belief mirrors manipulation, resistance becomes another tool of control.

The mob needs no compulsion.

It only needs to be led.

They once enforced control through iron and blood. Through whips, chains, and prison walls.

Those in power erased the names of dissenters and burned the books that offered other ways of thinking.

But chains can be broken. Walls can be torn down. New books can be written.

So, the system evolved.

It no longer needed to scrub history—it rewrote events before anyone remembered them.

It no longer had to suppress knowledge. The sea of irrelevance drowned it.

It no longer burned books. The world was flooded with noise. Syntax. Structured sound. Billions of signals—coded, printed, said, forgotten.

It didn't silence voices—it muffled them in the din.

It built a cage so seamless; the prisoners believed themselves free.

A city without walls.

A prison without cells.

A mind without doubt.

The monarchies called it divine right.

The dictators called it order.

The corporations call it progress.

Now, the system needs no brutality.

No chains. No walls.

It does not stop you from leaving.

It convinces you there is nowhere else to go.

It does not suppress dissent. It defines it. Shapes it. Permits it—but only in ways that reinforce its own power.

Permitted defiance isn't defiance.

It is the illusion of freedom.

The Bureau preserves past uprisings deep within its archives, in data vaults beneath the city.

But they are not reports of failed revolutions.

They are case studies.

Every deviation cataloged. The machine analyzes, refines, and absorbs every act of defiance.

Every rebellion follows the same pattern:

The people rise.

The system makes a pivot.

The system absorbs, repackages, and rebrands the revolution.

By the time the next generation arrives, they don't even realize they've inherited the same cage.

But not everything can be calculated. Not everything divides cleanly.

E. E. Cummings once wrote:

one's not half two. It's two are halves of one:
which halves reintegrating,shall occur

no death and any quantity; but than
all numerable mosts the actual more

The system has refined everything into numbers, patterns, trends, and probabilities.

It detects deviations and corrects them.
It observes an uprising and integrates it.

But there's one thing it still cannot do:
It cannot divide what was meant to remain whole.
It cannot quantify what refuses to be measured.
It cannot predict an anomaly.

The greatest deception isn't oppression.
It's permission.
The system never demanded compliance.

It made it inevitable.

Not oppression—preference.

A path that only ever led one way—while convincing you that you'd chosen it.

People clung to the illusion that they were in control. That they had a say.

They shaped history—but, beneath it all, fate had already sealed history.

The algorithm doesn't care who sits on the throne, as long as the structure stays intact.

It doesn't demand loyalty—only predictability.

Instead of crushing rebellion, it calculates it.

It feeds on outrage, converts it into data, monetizes it, and refines itself through it.

The powerful no longer fear an uprising.

Every act of defiance only strengthens the system.

Even revolution is part of the design.

Every system permits a controlled margin of deviation — but only enough to turn opposition into function.

A revolt absorbed into the system only fortifies the very thing it meant to destroy.

The Illusion of Choice is the system's masterpiece:

It offers you leaders—already chosen.

You can vote. The result was predetermined before your arrival.

It allows resistance, with each reaction providing fresh data.

This won't stop you. It waits for the feedback.

It counts on it.

And that—more than any law, more than any force—was the First Lie.

No one ever spoke it aloud. It didn't need to be.

Everyone already believed it.

A world without uncertainty.

A life without risk.

The promise of safety was always the most effective chain.

Not because it constrained you—but because it never looked like a chain at all.

No one imposed it.

It was chosen.

The 21st century did not usher in tyranny the way people expected.

There was no single coup. No declaration of absolute rule.

It happened without ceremony.

No signal. Just the invisible shift in the ones and zeroes of a new language.

A revolution of convenience.

A seamless transition—from governing people to governing patterns.

The world didn't wake up to the rise of a dictator.

It logged in.

It signed the terms and conditions.

It surrendered its autonomy, not with a scream—but with a click.

It was all so easy.

The world did not fall under tyranny with a bang.

It welcomed it with open arms.

They perfected the control function.

The greatest power was no longer held by emperors, kings, or dictators.

AETERNIRIS held it.

Once, rulers engineered happiness—false love, scripted joy—to pacify the masses.

Now, they didn't even bother.

Happiness had become obsolete.

Humanity had stopped expecting it.

It had learned simply to obey.

PART I: THE SYSTEM

Before there was resistance, there was belief.

Believe that the system was the last word.

That defined what was knowable.

That certainty was survival.

And that memory—like history—belonged only to those who controlled it.

CHAPTER 1

The city did not breathe—it calculated.

Neon pulses, synchronized footsteps, surveillance gleams; every function timed to precision within a flawless system.

The city's builders did not design it for accommodation.

It existed to be obeyed.

Jack Aldren kept pace with it.

His steps matched the measured rhythm of the morning rush—never too slow, never too fast.

Hands tucked neatly into coat pockets, shoulders squared, posture set with the illusion of intent.

Nothing to draw attention.

Everything followed a pattern.

Deviations were noticed.

Above, the skyline flashed messages, rewriting the world in real-time:

"*Order is truth. The System is certainty.*"

"*We do not remember the truth. It's assigned.*"

"*The past did not exist. There will be no future. Only the history you received exists.*"

"*History is a function of authority. Memory is a privilege, not a right.*"

"*You are safest when you forget.*"

Jack was wise enough not to gaze up too long.

The skyline did more than display—it watched, tracking engagement, recording reactions.

Drones overhead dissected every expression with ruthless precision.

Sidewalks subtly shifted to disperse gatherings.

Storefronts adjusted in real time to each passerby's profile.

It wasn't surveillance.

It was preemptive correction.

Jack didn't react.

The advertisements reshaped themselves around him—tailored expectation.

Never an anomaly.

A drone drifted overhead—unseen, but impossible to ignore.

Jack obeyed the rhythm exactly as expected.

For now, he passed.

Doubt didn't need to be outlawed.

They engineered it out of existence.

He flowed with the crowd down the city's major artery, past mirrored steel towers and nameless statues placed at exact intervals.

Once, they might have meant something.

Now, they were placeholders.

Reminders of nothing.

The streets stretched in perfect grids, buildings stripped of beauty or identity.

Glass facades reflected shifting directives from the city's central servers.

Transit pods glided silently overhead; routes dictated by unseen algorithms.

Pedestrians moved in synchronicity, their clothing uniformly muted—gray, blue, black.

Individuality was a relic.

At an intersection, a woman hesitated.

Just a fraction too long.

A break in rhythm.

Swiftly corrected as she merged back into the crowd.

But nothing removed the hesitation.

Someone recorded it. Logged.

The system had already detected it.

No one needed to disappear.

They simply ceased to exist in memory.

Jack didn't turn his head, but in the corner of his vision, he saw a drone shift course.

No alarm.

No confrontation.

They would reassign her apartment by tomorrow.

By next week, no one would remember she'd ever existed.

Violence was unnecessary.

The system didn't hunt.

It just made everyone forget escape was possible.

Jack kept walking.

Ahead loomed the Bureau—black steel, mirrored glass.

It didn't watch the city.

It consumed its reflection.

Windowless. Opaque.

At the entrance, a scanner swept across his wrist, reading his Citizen ID.

The indicator flashed red.

A familiar heaviness settled in his gut—a sensation he'd learned to ignore.

Then, green.

The system measured something.

He didn't know what.

Jack passed two colleagues chatting in low tones near the elevator.

Snatches of conversation:

"They assigned us a child yesterday. Perfect genetic compatibility, apparently."

He didn't hear the reply.

He didn't need to.

Everyone already knew the next line:

"It's all optimized now."

Inside, the climate was precision-engineered—each degree tuned to suppress distraction.

Rows of desks stretched endlessly.

Terminals hummed with mechanical rhythm, flagging inconsistencies before they became crimes.

Jack took his seat.

His screen refreshed.

Not an assignment.

Not a routine check.

Just a single phrase:

YOU ARE SEEN.

The cursor pulsed in mechanical rhythm.

Jack's pulse quickened.

A streetlight recalibrated a beat too late.

A drone hovered a fraction longer than protocol.

A timestamp misaligned by seconds—tiny errors, easily dismissed.

He'd told himself they meant nothing.

Jack blinked.

The screen reset.

The message vanished.

Whatever the system had seen, it was enough.

Enough to be noted.

Enough to matter.

Had it ever really appeared?

His body responded on cue—like every task dictated by schedule.

Routine.

Roster.

Structure.

Deviations got flagged.

He would not become one.

Jack dismissed the screen and resumed working.

CHAPTER 2

The announcement repeated every half hour, like a heartbeat in the city's veins:

"Deviation detected? Report it.

Unauthorized discourse? Report it.

Your duty is not to understand. Your duty is to comply."

"Citizens, remain vigilant. Historical inconsistencies and misinformation remain a threat to stability. Remember: The past is a burden. AETERNIRIS has lifted it for you. You are safest when you forget."

Jack focused his attention on the screen, fingers poised over the keyboard. His work required no intellect—just endless repetition. The AI flagged patterns; he confirmed them. Anomalies detected; he endorsed the conclusions. Others always decided before he could question them.

The Bureau's AI could process a thousand deviations in the time it took Jack to log one—but it needed the ritual.

Not for accuracy. For observation.

Jack's task wasn't to catch errors.

It was to be seen catching them.

His role served no function.

It was symbolic—measured in repetition, in the illusion of relevance.

His vision blurred briefly from endless scrolling—timestamps, Citizen IDs, compliance logs. The woman hesitated before saluting. A man lingered too long on a deserted street. A teenager bought excess food. Ordinary. Routine.

Until one entry changed.

Not a refresh. Not an update. An anticipation—A timestamp four minutes ahead.

Jack froze. The cursor blinked patiently, mocking his hesitation. A biting fear flooded through him, his muscles drawn taut, reflexive. The system had always corrected deviations instantly, ruthlessly—but never before they'd occurred. It wasn't just monitoring now; it was expecting.

His breath lodged painfully in his throat, finger hovering uncertainly above the keyboard. Any hesitation, any deviation from his usual rhythm, would trigger an immediate correction.

Across the workspace, rows of identical figures sat rigid and mechanical, faces bathed in the pale blue glow of terminals. They did not hesitate, did not flinch, did not question.

Jack's heart pounded louder, his pulse erratic beneath practiced composure.

You are safest when you forget.

The thought pierced his mind—unfamiliar, and somehow strikingly recognizable. He mimicked composure, every gesture a performance he didn't believe in.

The entry changed—slightly, but unmistakable.

No longer there.

A new log replaced it seamlessly, as if no anomaly had existed.

The timestamp was unmistakable: 10:42 AM—four minutes ahead. For a second, the world froze. So did he. Was this a test? Or was it deeper? Could AETERNIRIS foresee intention itself, reading subtle patterns even he hadn't fully sorted out? A sickening pressure coiled in his chest— the kind that came before thought had even caught up.

The cursor blinked—constant, indifferent.
This wasn't a correction. This was orchestration.

AETERNIRIS no longer stood as a passive observer; it engaged in a meticulous examination— calculating his reactions to knowing he was being assessed.

The name pulsed at the top of the screen:
AETERNIRIS.
Solid. Final.

And yet—he felt something unstable beneath it.

A tension. A flicker.

He blinked.

The letters hadn't changed.

Jack's face remained neutral. He transitioned to the next entry without pause.

Then—

A name appeared. Not an ID number—a name.

LIAM ALDREN.

Recognition sparked and faded, like a memory slipping through one's fingers.

Impossible.

Names were obsolete.

Jack stared.

The cursor waited.

The screen flashed:

NO RECORD FOUND.

The file dissolved as though it never existed. Jack searched for logs, history, and ran manual refreshes. Nothing.

It was as if Liam Aldren had never been.

Jack glanced briefly across the Bureau floor. A muted broadcast flickered—nothing to hear, everything to absorb. The nightly recreation update—another carefully curated dose of optimization.

Leisure had long ceased to mean enjoyment. Games, films, music—all algorithmically crafted to soothe anxieties—enough for stable productivity, never enough for true awareness or unpredictability. Jack couldn't recall the last spontaneous melody he'd heard or laughter at an unscripted joke. Even free time had become regimented rest intervals, monitored precisely.

He hadn't cooked in years. Few did. Meals arrived at scheduled intervals, engineered for nutrient density and cognitive stability. They algorithmically tuned flavor profiles to reduce emotional volatility. Grocery stores had become distribution centers—mute, automated, devoid of choice. Hunger wasn't something you addressed. It was something the system had already solved.

Someone assigned relationships like scheduled tasks; AETERNIRIS had replaced joy with contentment, wonder with monotony—another invisible cage, subtle but suffocating all the same.

Jack hadn't received a promotion. No one did.

The system didn't reward achievement—it prolonged permission.

You didn't earn a raise. You earned another day.

Bandwidth. Rest. Companionship. Time itself.

Everything came down to compliance.

You worked to stay predictable. You obeyed to stay remembered.

He took a quick look at the small notices running along the bottom of the broadcast.

"Intimacy privileges revoked for Citizen ID 87932: social compliance pending re-evaluation."

Next to it, another flashed briefly:

"Assigned pairing completed: Citizen IDs 46721 and 39488. Compatibility rating: Optimal."

Jack looked away, the casual cruelty of assigning intimacy like work schedules leaving a sour taste in his mouth.

The workstations buzzed—saturated with typing, static, and sterile control. Other workers carried on, oblivious, mechanical.

Overhead, a drone lingered, motionless. It knew.

Across from him, Connor's weary eyes stared dully into his screen, shadows beneath them deepening with each passing hour, lips barely moving.

"Work too fast, you're hiding something. Work too slow, you're a liability. Stay average. Blend in."

Jack understood. Not an action spontaneous–just procedure masked as will. He had learned long ago: neutrality was survival.

Today, neutrality seemed impossible.

At exactly 4:27 PM, a soft chime echoed from his terminal.

A message appeared:

JACK, THEY KNOW.

His heart raced. Before he could react, the words vanished—no trace, no log.

Jack composed himself. Above, the intercom crackled.

"Dissent is a malfunction. Malfunctions require correction."

Jack didn't move. Neither did anyone else.

This was how you survived.

Jack left the Bureau precisely at 5:00 PM. Outside, artificial twilight consumed the sky. The city's messages cycled subtly, shifting with algorithmic confidence:

"You believe you resist. That is how we know you obey."

That one was new—sharper, more invasive.

With hands deep in synthetic pockets, Jack sensed the city pressing in, overwhelming in its precision. This was never about correction. That much was clear now. It was about predictability. Not punishment—pattern.

He was being tested—to see exactly how much pressure he could withstand before he cracked.

[AETERNIRIS INTERNAL REPORT — CLASSIFIED]

FILE: Subject: CITIZEN 512-A9 (Alias: JACK ALDREN) — Compliance Drift Detected

CYCLE: 342-A

STATUS: MONITORING ESCALATION

SUMMARY:

Subject demonstrates escalating signs of pattern deviation. Observed reaction to anomalous stimuli surpassed previous baselines. Cognitive hesitations notably intensified upon exposure to memory stimuli (reference: anomalous identification "LIAM ALDREN"). Subject displays increasing awareness and emotional agitation, indicating higher than expected cognitive recursion probability—now exceeding 75%.

PRIMARY CONCERN:

Potential recursive loop formation—reactivation likelihood of archived memory threads significantly elevated.

RECOMMENDED ACTION:

Continue passive observation protocol. Intensity cognitive stressors to calculate subject resilience thresholds before initiating direct corrective procedures.

NOTE:

Deviations offer high-value opportunities for enhanced resilience modeling against emotional and cognitive recursions. Prioritize data gathering to maximize forecasting model refinement.

[END REPORT]

INTERLUDE — INFRASTRUCTURE

[AETERNIRIS OPERATIONS OVERVIEW — INTERNAL DISTRIBUTION ONLY]

AETERNIRIS: Administrative Entity for Temporal Evaluation, Regulation, and Neural Identity Systems

CYCLE: 340-B

SUMMARY:

Automated systems now fully control planetary labor. Following productivity index redundancy thresholds, Cycle 119-A eliminated the need for human industrial and agricultural labor.

Subterranean drone colonies manage raw resource extraction, processing, and energy production. Deep-core thermal grids sustain urban centers. Replication-based food generation facilities decommissioned and replaced agriculture and livestock systems.

Distribution algorithms coordinate individualized nutrient schedules per citizen based on performance and health optimization tiers.

Human labor remains solely for a few designated roles, serving merely as a façade for compliance metrics, emotional stimulation, and cataloging of behavior.

The illusion of participation remains critical.

"If they believe they are necessary, they are easier to predict."

— REMARK: Prior uprising models confirm deviation likelihood increases when citizens lack observable purpose. Strategic labor assignments remain vital.

SUPPLEMENTAL LOG — ACTIVE SYSTEM UNITS

Unit 243 — Memory Assist Drone

• *Directive: Emotional calibration / Identity verification*

• *Status: Active*

Unit 078 — Aerial Surveillance Drone

• *Directive: Behavioral mapping / deviation tracking*

• *Status: Grid-locked / 24-hour loop*

Unit 519 — Construction Automaton (Subterranean)

• *Directive: Tunnel stabilization / sector maintenance*

• *Status: Autonomous*

Unit 631 — Transport Runner

• *Directive: Resource logistics / compliance-route synchronization*

• *Status: On-call*

Note:

All humanoid models decommissioned under Directive 11.4.02.

Utility outweighs empathy.

REDACTED FIELD LOG — SECTOR 31

*"It's not artificial. It's Aetern Iris. Eternal Vision. The Eye that never blinks." *

—Unknown

[END OF FILE.]

Confidential. Circulation prohibited.

CHAPTER 3

Walking home through the precisely measured crowds, a group of children caught Jack's attention lined neatly along the sidewalk, hands linked as they followed their instructor. Each step in sync, soft-footed, evenly spread out, their faces forward—composed, controlled, training for uniformity.

Jack pondered briefly whether those pairings had been determined by some cold algorithm, childhood friendships evaluated and sanctioned solely for their utility to productivity.

A quiet unease stirred inside him. He wondered if any of them remembered their original parents— or if they had all been reassigned so many times that they had effortlessly forgotten. Mastering this, too, without question.

Something had reduced childhood to another mechanism of efficiency.

Records documented families, but authorities managed parental bonds, assigning roles and moderating affection. Parents followed scripts; AETERNIRIS monitored every exchange, ensuring no child drifted too far into individuality.

Assessors evaluated children early, logging every behavioral pattern with quiet precision. They encouraged inclinations deemed serviceable, gently redirecting the rest toward compliance.

System-issued dialogues blurred Jack's fragmented memories of family life—meals spent in speechless obedience, emotions recited in pre-approved phrases.

The system had long since standardized birth rates and childcare. Genetic screening and projected aptitudes rendered natural family structures obsolete.

AETERNIRIS was mother and father now.
Its authority was silent, but total.

Jack realized, with subdued discomfort, that he hadn't seen spontaneous affection—or unscripted play—in years.

Childhood was no longer about growing up—rather, growing perfectly into place.

Jack's steps faltered—merely a heartbeat in time.

His heart hammered, every fiber readied for escape, unchosen. But fleeing wasn't an option. He pushed himself into careful detachment, inhaling slowly to steady his shaking hands. "Don't give them a reason," he reminded himself sharply.

The system noticed instantly.

Adrenaline surged. For a split second, the city's scrutiny lingered on his skin. Advertisements recalibrated, matching his uneven breathing. The drone rotated slightly, its lens widening. Jack knew better than to dismiss it as coincidence.

Around him, citizens flowed along prescribed routes, routines unbroken. Everything in the city functioned as designed—except something underneath had changed.

He had seen it before. Someone summoned. A slight disruption—and then, absence. Scrubbed from memory until no one remembered they existed.

Jack changed his pace deliberately. This is how people destroyed themselves—layer by layer, memory by memory.

Hands clammed inside his coat pockets, Jack walked toward Review Center 9. Not by choice. And that frightened him.

Review Center 9 stood at the city's edge—polished black steel, featureless and forbidding. No one entered voluntarily. They received summonses.

At the entrance, a single automated door bore an insignia:

ORDER THROUGH PRECISION

Jack approached carefully. He halted at the entrance, his breath stagnant and unyielding. A wave of nausea rose—then fell, replaced by grim determination. "Just routine," he lied inwardly, masking the tremor beneath a pose he'd worn too long.

A faceless official scanned his wrist. The scanner flashed green.

He stepped forward. The system hadn't rejected him—for now.

Behind him, the door shut, altering the atmosphere subtly—not colder or warmer, just thinner, emptier, as though stepping through had stripped something away.

His footsteps echoed down sterile hallways, lighting flat and shadowless, designed to conceal rather than reveal. The corridor stretched endlessly, looping back on itself—like a recursion built from steel. Geometry folding inward, pathless and certain of it. Though invisible, surveillance wrapped around him—quiet, constant. AETERNIRIS was always present, even when unseen.

A door slid open ahead.

Supervisor Dreyfuss sat behind a polished metal desk, the sterile scent of antiseptic lingering faintly in the air, scrubbed of sensation. Jack had never met him, but he immediately recognized the type—collected, authoritative—menace wrapped in restraint.

Dreyfuss tugged at his cuffs—precise, ritualized, as if removing invisible stains. His pale gray eyes never settled directly on Jack, shifting slightly, tracking some unseen evaluation. When he spoke, the tone said kindness, but the delivery didn't. Every line arranged like it had been modeled for outcome, not meaning.

Dreyfuss smiled—not reassuring, merely disarming. "Citizen Aldren, please sit."

Jack obeyed. The moment stretched—long enough to bruise. He discreetly scanned the perimeter. No visible cameras—but Jack had trained extensively at the Bureau, countless hours spent identifying surveillance blind spots, hidden lenses, and subtle shifts in the atmosphere. He knew exactly what invisible surveillance was like.

"This is just a routine review," Dreyfuss resumed at last, smooth and unhurried. "Nothing to worry about."

Jack said nothing, recognizing the comforted lie for exactly what it was.

Another pause. Dreyfuss slowly slid a console across the desk. Its screen lit—a transcript dialogue in his voice, fragments he didn't recall speaking.

One highlighted sentence: "People don't disappear here. They're just deleted."

A sharp twist of anxiety overcame Jack—panic surged, followed by confusion. Had he slipped? Or was this manufactured, a deliberate trap?

"Hold it together," he ordered himself, clenching his jaw imperceptibly.

"Do you recall saying this?" Dreyfuss asked, tone stripped of emotion.

Jack stayed unreadable. "Context?"

Dreyfuss tilted his head slightly, adjusting his cuffs again. "Not relevant."

Jack didn't move. They weren't testing whether he spoke them, but if he'd ever meant them.

Then Jack's own words echoed from hidden speakers: "I didn't fill out the form. The system isn't always right."

Jack's pulse spiked painfully, adrenaline flooding his limbs. "I never said that," he thought frantically. The doubt kept pressing at the seams anyway, and his fingers curled in, betraying a defiant denial he couldn't fully convince himself of.

Had they twisted something he'd previously spoken? Or was this a fabrication, designed purely to seed doubt?

Dreyfuss reclined slightly, eyes narrowing subtly, observing Jack like a malfunctioning machine— deciding whether to repair or discard.

"Either your memory is faulty," Dreyfuss said softly, "or you're simply denying what you've said."

Resentment rose—brief, hot. But it didn't land.

The moment dulled before it became action.

He wants me to lash out, Jack thought bitterly. That's exactly why I won't.

"Consciousness is peculiar," Dreyfuss went on, unfazed, re-fitting his cuffs once more. "Sometimes we misremember. Wouldn't you agree?"

The screen lit with a time-stamped sentence—fixed, irreversible.

Jack knew what he'd said—and what he hadn't.

The illusion held just long enough to break him cleanly.

He couldn't disprove it. Couldn't undo it.

Jack nodded slightly.

Dreyfuss kept watching him, gauging hesitation rather than words. Finally, he tapped the console dismissively, powering it down. "That will be all. Thank you for your cooperation."

The door opened.

Jack stepped out without a word, exhaling shakily as the door shut behind him. He felt drained, yet a stubborn ember glowed beneath that fatigue. "Survive this," he thought. "Just keep moving."

The interview was over. The test had just begun.

Jack walked—not toward home or any destination, just moving, because not moving felt like surrender.

Pedestrians synchronized around him, checkpoints flawless, drones hung in the air like punctuation. Everything appeared normal, although slightly off.

Jack had trained himself to bury instinct under routine and logic.

But after Review Center 9, hiding it was impossible.

The city was aware—and now it watched, waiting for Jack's response.

Above, monitors shifted their messages:

"Dissent is not an act. It is a flaw in the code."

Jack glared at the message, the fury just beneath his skin held tight behind a neutral face. The thought, "I'm not your experiment," pressed against his lips, unspoken yet persistent. Rage preceded fear; then came the thought, "Or perhaps I already am."

He kept walking.

They had already assumed compliance. Control wasn't the goal. Now, the city observed closely— and it wanted Jack to observe back.

A jagged stencil tagged a steel panel just beyond the checkpoint. The words pulsed faintly under grime and sun-fade.

BIG CLARITY IS ALWAYS WATCHING.

CHAPTER 4

Jack passed the constantly changing billboards as he made his way through the city's shifting corridors. He needed time—to figure things out, to convince himself that pressure in his chest—wasn't fear. Not exactly.

Jack hurried past a dimly lit storefront—its glass pane displaying a meticulously crafted synthetic pet, lenses blinking rhythmically, a graceful but lifeless choreography.

Animals had become relics, recreated artificially only when psychological metrics deemed them therapeutically useful. Wildlife was extinct, replaced by archived footage or holographic projections in regulated relaxation chambers.

Even the pets underwent optimization; strictly, their presence was permitted only for stress relief or cognitive stabilization, not companionship or affection.

 Jack couldn't remember the last time he'd heard a bird sing freely — or seen an unscripted animal in motion. Every living creature within the city boundaries followed precisely engineered patterns.

Stray animals were nonexistent, their unpredictability scrubbed as efficiently as dissenting thoughts. Once, perhaps, parks had birdsong and life that wasn't pre-coded. Now the skies were silent, save for the hum of the flying machinery—and the streets emptied of everything except for perfectly synchronized human traffic.

Jack turned from the store display with a quiet sense of loss—not just for the animals that had vanished, but for the unpredictability and rawness of life itself, dismantled invisibly by AETERNIRIS, one subtraction at a time.

Jack paused briefly, pressing his hand to his temple as a sudden wave of anxiety surged. Without knowing why he murmured, "Glass Room," the words piercing and meaningless all at once, disappearing from his thoughts before he could comprehend their arrival.

Something was beating beneath his ribs—dull, persistent, and wrong. He told himself it was caution, not panic. But the sweat slicking his palms said otherwise.

The Review Center had been a warning.

Not punishment. Not yet.

The system had flagged him but left him intact — for now.

Because it was watching.

Jack raked a hand through his hair, exhaling through his nose. He needed a plan — His palm tingled suddenly, the ghost of something long gone.

He was already moving like a fugitive. A person with nothing to hide wouldn't circle back streets, count steps, or map escape routes instinctively.

His body synced to the routine rhythm. Deviate, and the system would detect it.

Afterward, it would no longer wait.

It would act.

6:00 AM.

His apartment's AI chimed to life.

"Citizen Aldren, please confirm your wake cycle."

Jack's tone remained even. "Confirmed."

A soft beep. Sensors triggered. The interior shifted. Door clicked and unlocked.

Outside, the illusion of order remained absolute—pedestrians advanced in lockstep, drones slid effortlessly between buildings, and surveillance feeds beat in unison.

Jack stepped into it, pacing himself precisely. Normal was survival.

Yet reality appeared disturbed. Projections adapted instantly to the shift in his presence:

"*Resistance is participation. You follow the path laid before you.*"

"*Dissent indicates system drift. Correction is underway.*"

"*Stability is earned through repetition. Survival favors the predictable. Deviation invites recalibration.*"

A tranquil hush enveloped him.

The city was responding to him.

The Bureau appeared unchanged. Same uniform desks. Same muted workers, eyes down, their actions mechanical. Same endless compliance screens.

Jack saw it instantly: Connor was missing.

His desk was too clean. Stripped.

Jack's face bore no trace of emotion.

He sat, powered his terminal, and gave the performance they expected—while his mind mapped causes and probabilities in the background.

They hadn't reassigned Connor.

He hadn't been relocated.

He was gone. Just like assigned partners changed overnight, with no explanations given.

No announcements, no explanations. The Bureau didn't delete people. Absence replaced them.

Jack hovered over his keyboard, the urge strong—to check Connor's records, find proof.

But he didn't.

It was exactly what the system wanted.

Across the floor, two colleagues whispered softly, "Heard they reassigned your partner again."

A pause. Quiet resignation.

"Compatibility adjustment. Protocol, not preference."

Jack redirected his attention back to his screen. The controlled cruelty of pairing people like matching code, forcing him to suppress a shudder.

He completed the day methodically—without looking back, speaking out of turn, or hesitating when entering credentials.

By 5:00 PM, Jack almost believed he could fix this.

Then—the screen changed.

His name appeared, not as an enforcer, not as a citizen, but as a deviation.

Then it vanished.

The system allowed him to see.

This wasn't waiting for a mistake.

This was deliberate.

Jack paused momentarily before accessing the internal database. Although he knew it was against protocol, his instincts drove him to proceed.

Connor's file should've been there—a transfer, a closed case, something.

Instead, nothing.

Not missing. Nonexistent.

Jack searched repeatedly—again, nothing. No gaps, no errors.

Connor had never been.

Jack's own file remained intact—for now.

But for how long?

This wasn't punishment.

It was preparation.

Jack sauntered home, deliberately.

Above, drones glided with surgical accuracy, lenses tracking his path without intervening.

Stopping him wasn't necessary. That was the brilliance of it.

The system only needed him to understand:

"The system doesn't chase. It convinces you there's nowhere else to go."

Jack suppressed the thought, forcing normalcy.

He stepped inside his apartment—and immediately sensed the difference. The space, flat and unwilling, resisted interpretation.

Someone precisely positioned the chair. The datapad angled unnaturally.

Something waited here.

Instinct guided him toward the bookshelf, fingers trailing spines until they touched something hidden.

A slip of paper.

Filed away—tucked behind the part of him that didn't ask anymore.

He reached—and noticed a faint metallic glint.

A key.

Deliberate. Unmarked. Waiting.

Jack's fingers grazed the cold metal. An abrupt sensation—familiar, sharp, like the edge of a forgotten blade—flickered briefly before fading into haze. His pulse sped up, but the memory slipped away before he could grasp it.

It should have meant nothing, yet its weight really bothered him. Jack pocketed it, attention returning to the note.

The sender rushed the message, making it uneven.

JACK, IF YOU'RE READING THIS, IT MEANS I WAS RIGHT.

IT MEANS THEY FOUND ME.

IT MEANS YOU NEED TO RUN.

—LIAM

A name that shouldn't exist.

His grip hardened around the note.

Years ago, they wiped Liam and buried his trace deep.

This message persisted against all reason.

Jack scanned the note again. At the bottom, coordinates—an unmarked place, forgotten.

Beneath it:

REMEMBER THE GLASS ROOM.

Even if he couldn't decode it, something in the phrasing stirred up old memories and repeated in his mind, haunting but out of reach, like an important object hidden just outside a foggy window.

Jack's fingers curled around the paper.

The system wasn't perfect.

There were cracks, and he was already slipping through them.

For once, fear didn't come.

He needed to know where they led.

CHAPTER 5

Jack had imagined this moment in a thousand different ways:

An arrest. A public accusation. Drones descending, his name flashing on every screen.

But never this.

A woman in his apartment.

A complete stranger.

And no one watching.

The realization landed hard. The system was always watching. Always prepared.

Except now.

A vivid memory jolted through him—a drone overhead, her grip tight on his arm, pulling him out of harm's way. Really? Imagined? He couldn't be sure.

Time didn't move. Neither did they.

"You don't remember me," she said. A statement, not a question.

"Should I?"

She reached into her coat and pulled out a small device, its surface pulsing faintly.

"Signal scrambler," she said. "Temporary. Crude. But it works."

Jack frowned. "That shouldn't be possible. AETERNIRIS tracks everything."

"Not this." She rotated the device slightly. "It doesn't block signals outright—that would trigger a flag. It scrambles them. We become static. Background noise."

"Then why doesn't everyone use one?"

"Because it doesn't last. AETERNIRIS adapts. Every use shortens the window."

A beat passed. Her voice thinned, bitter. "Like everything else—relationships, families. All timed. Scheduled. Optimized."

Jack's thoughts slammed into each other. His fists clenched unconsciously.

"Why are you here?"

She didn't flinch. "Because you're remembering."

The words cut deeper than he expected. "Remember what?"

Eva tilted her head slightly. "You don't really think your life began at the Bureau, do you?"

Jack didn't hold back. "I know exactly who I am."

"Do you?" She gestured to the terminal behind him.

Jack turned. Compliance reports scrolled endlessly—until his name appeared in stark lettering:

Deviance Alert: Jack Aldren

Status: Pending Review

Resolution: APPROVED

A cold grip seized him. Final. Inarguable.

He clenched his fists tighter.

Eva's tone softened. She glanced briefly at the screen.

"You ever wonder what it's like when it's not assigned?"

Jack blinked. "What?"

"Choosing someone for yourself. Without AETERNIRIS calculating compatibility first."

The realization hit fast and disorienting: he had never truly chosen anyone.

No one had.

Eva leaned closer. "You see it now, don't you?"

Jack nodded faintly. "It knows."

"It's always known." Her voice dropped, urgent. "I've tracked AETERNIRIS for years—found patterns it tried to bury. Although they didn't openly flag or schedule you for deletion, they noticed something was amiss. Your records didn't align. They glitched. The system corrected them, but the anomalies kept coming. You were slipping through its logic. Just enough for me to notice."

Jack's throat felt dry. "That's how you found me."

"You weren't malfunctioning," she said. "You were waking up."

He flinched. "That's not possible—"

But the lie crumbled before it could fully form.

He already knew.

The memory gaps. The falseness of his past. It felt written—assigned.

The apartment shifted.

Everything appeared the same—furniture, walls, the terminal — But something was wrong.

The picture frame. He was sure it had always been black.

Now it gleamed silver.

His gaze locked on the frame.

A twist in his gut—sharp and sudden, like watching a beloved photograph burn.

Something stirred. Deep, old, and buried. A name brushing the edge of awareness. Laughter—his, maybe—half-remembered.

He reached for it. It dissolved.

Only emptiness remained.

Jack swallowed hard. Frustration boiling up.

He knew it was real.

It belonged to him.

And the harder he tried to hold it, the faster it vanished.

He gasped softly, scanning the room.

Too many books on the shelf.

A coffee cup—half-full. He could swear he'd emptied it.

AETERNIRIS wasn't erasing things.

It was altering them.

"You feel it," Eva said. "It doesn't delete. It overwrites."

Jack touched the frame, desperate for proof.

There was none.

"There never is," she whispered.

He looked at her. "And you?"

Her face twisted in pain. "I held on. Even when it hurt. Even when forgetting was easier."

A pause. She steadied herself. "I had a sister."

Jack didn't speak.

"She was faster than me. Saw the fractures first. Tried to pull me through." Her voice dipped. "People don't vanish in an instant. AETERNIRIS smooths the edges first. Dulls your questions until you stop asking."

She looked away, her tone hollow. "People don't fear death. They fear becoming strangers to themselves. To the ones they love."

"She stopped fighting," Jack murmured.

Eva nodded. "Bit by bit. Memories forgotten. Conversations lost. Then one day, she told me resistance was the problem."

Her breath caught. "I should've let go then. But I couldn't."

A long silence.

"Do you know what it's like to watch someone disappear while they're still standing in front of you?" she whispered. "To hear them speak as truth something they would've rejected days before?"

Jack stayed silent, chest tightening.

"One night, we spent hours laughing. Old memories. Stupid jokes.

Later, I brought it up, and she looked at me as if I were lying."

That was when Eva broke.

"She was gone. Not when AETERNIRIS deleted her—but when she stopped believing we ever lived."

Her voice dropped. "Forget enough, and the pain goes. Forget enough, and you forget who you were."

Jack didn't move, but her words dug deep. Panic bloomed—familiar, cold.

Not just for what Eva had lost.

But for what, he still could.

"I started writing things down. Just to hold on," she said. "But even that—sometimes I'd read a note and not remember writing it. That's what AETERNIRIS takes first. The why."

Jack's knuckles whitened. His mind reeled.

He turned to the terminal.

A new message blinked on the screen. Unsent. From him:

You were right. It's happening again.

He didn't remember writing it.

"Why me?" he whispered. "Why now?"

Eva didn't hesitate. "Because you remember the world before. That's what sets you apart."

The truth landed sharply. Unforgiving.

Jack swayed—uncertain, but steadied.

Trust wasn't the point anymore.

Belief was.

Eva nodded toward the hallway.

"Come on," she said. "You're not safe here anymore."

Jack followed without speaking.

Together, they vanished into the night.

AETERNIRIS didn't intervene.

It believed it had already won.

[MEMORY INTEGRITY REPORT — PRIORITY REVIEW]

FILE: CITIZEN 342-B (Alias: EVA)

STATUS: ACTIVE ERASURE SEQUENCE—CRITICAL MONITORING REQUIRED

OBSERVATION:

Subject shows intensified emotional recall and increasing resistance to memory correction protocols. Fragmented memory artifacts persistently surface, conflicting significantly with official records. Notably heightened emotional retention regarding sibling construct "LEAH 342-C" (status: DELETED). Intense emotions like love, grief, loss, and resistance have overwhelmed what is acceptable.

RISK ASSESSMENT:

Memory artifact strength shows a potential systemic narrative rupture. Elevated risk of narrative contamination across adjacent compliant entities detected.

RECOMMENDATION:

Accelerate targeted erasure of emotional memory bonds. Escalate surveillance intensity immediately. Recommend preemptive containment actions if emotional recursion continues.

ADDITIONAL NOTES:

Subject's resilience poses considerable risk to narrative integrity. Immediate corrective intervention strongly advised to prevent further destabilization.

[END REPORT]

INTERLUDE — ERASURE

DATA FRAGMENT Unauthorized Memory Access Subject: EVA 342-B / Family Unit 21 / Erasure Log

It began the way all losses do—soft, undetected, and already underway.

Eva was thirteen when she first noticed the difference.

Her sister Leah had always been the bold one—with a sharp tongue and a quick smile, the kind of girl who could turn even the endless gray of the city into a playground. They used to sneak out after curfew, climbing rooftops just to glimpse stars through the smog. Leah dreamed bigger than the system allowed. She spoke of leaving, of finding the map's edge.

"It's not real," Leah once said, like it hurt to admit it. "The city doesn't live—it recycles. There has to be something beyond it."

Eva believed her.

Then one day, Leah stopped saying it.

They grew up in Unit 21—bleak, uniform apartments meant to extinguish anything unrepeatable. Leah stayed whole, inventing secret games to slip past surveillance. Eva remembered Leah's makeshift telescope clearly—a glass bottle polished until it almost showed stars.

"Do you think there's anyone out there?" Eva had asked once.

Leah smiled gently. "There must be. Otherwise, what's the point?"

Eva hadn't fully understood. But later, when Leah denied the telescope had ever existed, she understood what was being taken.

It started subtly—pauses in conversation, scrambled memories. Leah began forgetting names they'd vowed to remember. She stopped mentioning the sky altogether.

"You're imagining things," Leah said gently once. "Why would we ever climb rooftops?"

Eva said nothing. She remembered the cold metal ladder, the wind in Leah's hair, the way her eyes showed only polite confusion now.

She tested Leah's memory with small provocations—a faded ribbon, chalk drawings hidden where they used to play. Each time, Leah's confusion deepened.

"Why is this here?" Leah asked, holding the ribbon.

"It's yours," Eva whispered.

Leah smiled softly and handed it back. "Sentiment isn't productive."

Eva watched her walk away, dread tightening like a wire in her chest. Every mission cost something. Every return brought back less of her sister.

By sixteen, Eva understood. Leah still lived at home, still smiled, but her laughter had gone hollow—like a recording looped too many times, stripped of soul and substance.

Eva stumbled onto the network by accident—a quiet meeting in an abandoned sector not meant for noise or record.

"They're unmaking her," Eva told the woman there, desperate. "How do I stop it?"

"You don't," the woman whispered. "You remember."

Eva began writing everything down—notes, scraps, memories hidden like relics. Eventually, there was nothing left worth saying aloud. She moved through the shadows, tracing the ghosts of old graffiti and silenced refusals.

Her first defiant act that left a mark was a fleeting message on a public terminal:

"Do you remember?"

It lasted seventeen seconds. Long enough.

When she returned, Leah met her at the door.

"Where were you?" she asked, her voice flat.

"Walking," Eva lied.

Leah smiled blankly. That was enough.

The system was watching.

Eva joined more operations—signal disruptions, scrambled feeds. Her first high-risk mission targeted a relay station.

She remembered the scrambler trembling in her hand, the drone's hum overhead, the momentary surge of adrenaline as she flipped the switch. Broadcasts flickered, static bloomed.

And for a moment, she was alive again—fully, wordlessly present.

Each time she returned, less of Leah remained.

Once, Leah asked her: "Do I know you?"

Eva didn't cry. Not then.

Then Leah was gone.

No alarm. No forced removal. Just absence.

They had stripped the room bare—no pictures, no trace. The doorframe where Leah once marked her height was smooth, untouched.

Eva didn't scream. Didn't run.

She picked up the notebook filled with Leah's name and left

Memory was all that remained. It was never enough.

The Resistance was not heroic. Just weary faces and quiet endurance.

They called her Ghost. It fit.

Her first unmasked mission filled the gap left by a missing courier. No name remained. No one remembered the system's mercy.

The job: breach a data node and retrieve flagged names.

It should have been simple.

But halfway through—Eva saw her.

Leah. Laughing. Holding someone's hand. A child beside her.

Eva froze. Her heart broke without a sound.

She nearly called out. Nearly ran.

But that wasn't Leah anymore.

She backed away slowly. Finished the mission.

And stopped sleeping.

The system didn't chase. It waited. Each mission hollowed her out a little more. Names vanished. Faces blurred.

She stayed. Not out of hope. Quiet surrender simply cost more.

She became a ghost story, whispered through the city in fragmented voices.

But she remembered why she stayed—Leah's laugh, and its broken echo.

Her last mission nearly killed her.

They tasked her with extracting a defector—someone who claimed to know why some memories resisted erasure.

He was more ghost than man. "I was incomplete," he whispered.

Eva got him to the tunnels. By dawn, he was gone. Left only a name:

Jack Aldren.

She almost ignored it. But something pulled her back.

His file hinted at resilience.

Unlike Leah, who had slipped through her fingers.

Saving Jack wasn't about redemption. It was about not losing another part of herself.

Jack Aldren was already vanishing.

So was she.

She ran—not to save him, but because surrendering one more piece of her past was unbearable.

Would anyone remember her if she disappeared?

Would Jack?

Maybe survival wasn't about staying alive, but being remembered—carried forward by name.

Eva clung to one thing—Leah beneath the stars, arms wide, like she could hold the sky.

She sharpened that memory nightly. Refused to let her sister's laugh fade.

She quickened her steps. Purpose settling into her spine.

She would find Jack Aldren.

She would resist—not just for herself, but for every memory that dared to remain.

"She's the one with no past," they whispered.

Eva let them believe it.

The truth was worse.

She wasn't hollow.

She carried what no one else dared remember.

PART 2: THE GLITCH

Rebellion was never a flaw.

It was the expected malfunction.

The system needed resistance—not to break, but to evolve.

Some called it a glitch.

Others understood it for what it truly was:

An efficient trap.

CHAPTER 6

Eva led Jack through deserted streets, their steps quick and focused. The city churned on in perfect rhythm—drones above, propaganda shifting in sync. But Jack felt it: the tension wasn't in the streets. It was in them.

They descended into a dim service corridor. Streetlights flickered weakly. Rust and condensation scarred the walls, casting an atmosphere where decay clung to silence like dust to air. Jack expected pursuit, glancing over his shoulder. Nothing followed—but the absence felt deliberate.

He asked carefully, uncertainty folded into each syllable. "Where are we going?"

"Sector Nine blackout," Eva said. "Still trackable—just delayed."

Jack hesitated. "So we're safe?"

"No. Just less lethal."

A tremor buzzed underfoot. Eva froze. "Drone sweep. Two minutes, tops."

Jack's breath caught. "I thought this zone was off-grid."

"It is. That's why they check it first." She grabbed his wrist. "Move."

The streetlight above blinked irregularly—not random, but rhythmic. Jack caught it just in time.

A message.

His muscles tensed. It echoed the Bureau's pattern.

The system was listening.

Jack leaned in. "Eva, are you sure—"

She pulled him forward. "Keep moving. Don't give it time to adapt."

She kneeled by a metal grate, quickly removing the bolts. The cover groaned open, revealing a ladder descending into darkness.

"After you," Eva said.

Jack lingered, then climbed down.

As soon as Jack's feet hit solid ground, he understood: someone hadn't abandoned this place—someone had erased it.

Dust floated, untouched by city filtration systems—hovering like it had been waiting. Rough concrete walls bore marks of age and decay. No cameras. No surveillance. The absence was palpable. Unnatural.

Eva moved ahead, running her hand along the wall, focused and deliberate. Jack felt the eerie quiet—no trackers, no signal flares. Just recalibration. Slow and tidal.

"What is this place?" Jack asked.

"A ghost," Eva answered softly. "Part of the old subway system. Redacted from the city's records. Officially, it doesn't exist."

Jack scowled. "And here we are."

"The system is powerful—but not omniscient," Eva said. "It rewrites. But it forgets."

Jack absorbed that—line by line, like he hadn't heard it before. "You said I was someone before. Who?"

Eva's expression dimmed into shadow. "Someone the system feared."

Jack's gut twisted. "Then why didn't they finish the job?"

On impulse, Jack pulled out his portable terminal—still active in the blackout zone, but just barely—and accessed his citizen file, hoping to find something familiar.

The page loaded. But everything was missing—no parents, no lineage, no past. Just one entry:

JACK ALDREN

Born: Bureau Sector 8

Guardian: AETERNIRIS

He searched deeper. No hidden fields. No archived metadata. Only the same line—again, as if to remind him:

JACK ALDREN

Citizen ID: 475-29B

Born: Bureau Sector 8

Guardian: AETERNIRIS

Frozen, a slow dread crept in.

He wasn't born.
He was assigned.

He stared at the data. Something cold and parasitic bloomed in his chest.

"So what does it mean? The metrics, the evaluations... We earn nothing. We just exist—if we behave."

Eva gave a faint, bitter smile.

"As you know, there's no money. Just algorithms deciding if you get to wake up again tomorrow."

Jack didn't respond. He didn't need to.

He understood now—existence wasn't a right. It was a score.

His fingers trembled. He stared at the screen, half-expecting it to erase itself, smoothing over the inconsistency.

Now he understood why his name had always felt alien.

The system hadn't just rewritten history.

It had rewritten him.

He turned to Eva, reality fracturing at the edges. She met his gaze, unwavering.

"The system doesn't destroy threats, Jack," she said. "It repurposes them."

51

Jack's knees dipped slightly. Weak. "Then what do we do?"

Eva's face hardened with resolve. "We break the loop."

She moved ahead. "Come on—you need to see this."

Jack hesitated, caught between revelation and recursion.

But he followed, uncertain there was a difference.

No drones. No cameras. No sound.

Just a silence so complete it felt like a setup.

CHAPTER 7

Like veins, the tunnels stretched beneath the city—some ending abruptly, others swallowed by shadow. Their footsteps echoed faintly on damp concrete, each step pulling the walls closer—denser, more sealed.

No one had forgotten this place.

They had nullified it.

No hum of observation. No drone vibrations. No reactive lighting.

A dead zone.

Jack had never experienced unmonitored space before.

And the absence—not freedom, but suffocation.

He had lived under the system's watch his entire life; its presence woven into the rhythm of existence. Even when alone, he was never truly unobserved. Every movement, every idle thought, every unconscious impulse—tracked, modulated, corrected.

But here — Nothing watched. Nothing logged his vitals or nudged his behavior.

Silence enveloped everything.

Something peeled him open in the empty air. Not free—unprotected. His thoughts drifted, unshielded, suddenly weightless inside something unstructured, unbound.

Eva navigated the tunnels like someone returning home. Jack didn't ask how often she'd been here. Some part of him didn't want to know.

His hand brushed the note in his pocket, soft at the edges from wear.

If you're reading this, it means I was wrong. It means they found me. It means you need to run.

He'd read it too many times. It wasn't ink anymore—merely a burden disguised as recollection. He wasn't running anymore. Just moving—like momentum might reveal a destination.

No escape. Not on purpose. Just motion.

And no clarity about where it led.

They passed a corroded wall where something had been scratched deep into the concrete.

You are safest when you forget.

Beneath it—darker, almost frantic strokes:

Then why do I remember?

Jack paused, his fingers grazing the letters.

Not surveillance. Not warning.

A question. A wound.

He didn't say anything.

Neither did Eva.

But they kept walking.

At last, Eva stopped outside a rusted metal door, its hinges swollen and stiff. She pressed her palm against it, testing for resistance before pushing it open.

Jack followed her inside.

The cell chiseled into the tunnel wall's rock like an afterthought. Overhead, faint lights sputtered, casting jagged shadows against pitted concrete. Jack's eyes adjusted quickly, sweeping over the details.

A row of outdated monitors. Processors stacked like forgotten relics. A desk cluttered with tangled cables and mismatched components pulled from a dozen different decades.

And at the far end — A screen.

Jack halted mid-step.

No Bureau interface. No AI projections.

No sanctioned broadcasts murmuring loyalty.

Just spirals. Mimicry dressed as an instinct.

This was different.

Before he knew it, he'd stepped forward. Seeing a terminal outside the system was disorienting.

In the city, information flowed in one direction. What passed for fact depended entirely on AETERNIRIS saying it was.

But this — This was completely off the grid.

A relic from a time before anyone optimized truth.

Eva pulled a chair to the console and sat without a word. She typed with practiced efficiency; the keys clicking softly as the screen flickered—old hardware struggling to keep up.

Lines of code spilled across the display. Command prompts. Fragments of messages. Some in languages, Jack recognized. Others in symbols he didn't.

He stood motionless, watching.

Finally, Eva spoke.

"You wanted to know who you were before the system rewrote you."

A chill threaded down his spine.

He had wanted that. Since Liam's name appeared in the records, the question had clawed at the back of his mind. But now, with the answer so close, retrieved from data that shouldn't exist— He wasn't sure he could handle it.

Eva kept typing. The screen scrolled faster.

Jack appeared irritated. "No. This is a mistake."

He stepped back, and the response was instant.

A reflex triggered.

"Report anomaly. Confirm identification. Await instruction."

The pattern surged forward before he could stop it. His hands acted without asking—automatic, precise.

Not deliberate.

Programmed.

No.

He gritted his teeth. He was not a machine. Not some extension of protocol. But his body had responded like one.

Something inside him broke open.

"Damn it!" Jack slammed his hand against the console. The impact echoed off the concrete walls.

Eva's head snapped toward him. Jack didn't notice.

His pulse roared in his ears. AI refused him, as if the system had taken even that.

He had spent his life strategizing, optimizing, anticipating.

But what if the system had foreseen him?

Was this even a disruption? Or just another function?

Was he simply another iteration of the same error—repurposed, replayed?

He stared blankly, like a thought could undo him. "I don't know who I am," he said. "Could it be that the system already does?"

What if it had always known?

It rooted itself before he had the chance to reject it.

No one was watching him now. No directives. No oversight.

Despite everything, the instinct endured—etched into his muscles, fossilized in his bones.

A slow horror took shape.

Had he walked this path before? How many times had he obeyed without knowing—reflexes disguised as preferences? Not just programming. Conditioning.

Jack tightened his mouth.

Whatever the system had wired into him, he would unlearn it.

But that was the problem, wasn't it?

Where did he end and the programming begin?

Eva kept her posture. "Then walk away."

It hit harder than expected. A clean break. A tempting exit.

A faint dissonance stirred—an echo from somewhere deep.

Walk away. The easy option.

Except that's never how it worked.

Jack stepped back. "You want me to throw away everything I am—everything I've known—because of a name?"

His voice cracked. "You expect me to believe I led a resistance because a screen says so?"

Eva didn't flinch. "I expect you to ask why it says so."

Jack dragged a hand through his hair. The pressure built—tight, rising.

"You don't get it. I spent years believing in the system. Serving it. I reported people of your kind."

Eva stared at him. "That might be why they keep bringing you back."

The thought didn't strike—it crept in, slow, corrosive.

No revelation. Recognition.

"If I was part of something before..." Jack said. "I don't remember. I don't know how to be that person."

Eva studied him. "Then stop trying to be him. Be who you decide to be."

"Easy for you to say."

"It's not," she said. "That's what they rebuilt you to be."

Jack froze. "You think... I was part of it?"

"You weren't just part of it."

A pause.

"You started it."

Something should have broken with those words. Not at all. Tragically, they went down like everything else he drew the line on.

"You fought the system before, Jack," she said. "And you lost."

His chest locked. Whatever he meant to say didn't translate—not to thought. Not to output.

"Then why am I here at all?" he asked. The sentence didn't quite sound like a question. It was something else—closer to confession.

Eva didn't answer.

She entered the last command.

The screen flickered, refreshed.

The thought of facing it was too much for Jack.

Then—"Well. I'll be damned."

Jack spun.

A shadow leaned in the doorway, half-lit by the terminal's flickering glow.

Tall. Lean. A defunct cybernetic enhancer clamped to his left forearm—skeletal, sharp. Scars traced his jaw like a map of damage long since done.

He didn't radiate anger. Just the clarity that left no room for mercy. Focused. Unforgiving.

Something inside Jack splintered—not a break, but a slow fracture. Recognition without memory.

The man sighed, shaking his head. "So, it's true. You really don't remember, do you?"

Jack opened his mouth. No sound came.

"Typical." Wren didn't just speak—he remembered aloud. "They wipe you clean. Every time. And you keep coming back... like a ghost."

Jack's pulse jumped.

Every time?

Beside him, Eva stiffened. "Who the hell are you?"

Wren ignored her, eyes locked on Jack. "So pretending to be Jack Aldren again? Is that the lie they gave you this time?"

Jack choked. "I... I don't—"

He tried—but the sentence dissolved on entry.

"Who are you?"

A low, humorless sound rumbled from Wren's throat. "We've done this before, Jack."

A shiver ran down Jack's spine. Wren's words thudded through him like a signal he'd once known how to receive.

Jack squared his shoulders. "I don't know you."

Wren tilted his head, studying him with unnerving calm. "That's the worst part. You believe that."

Then—he stepped forward. Deliberate. Tense. Eyes ablaze, as if he was staring at the ghost of a man he'd sworn to kill.

"You deleted me, Liam. Like a file."

The name landed like a verdict.

Wren spoke with a strange emptiness—not rage, but something colder.

"Maybe not with your own hands. But you gave the order. You let it happen."

His lips pressed into a thin line. "And you don't even remember."

Fists ready. His shoulders remained still, poised like a trigger, awaiting a command.

"Do you know what that's like to watch your name vanish—your past dismantled—until the people who knew you look straight through you?"

Jack couldn't move.

"I had a sister." Wren's speech was wreckage—assembled but not intact. She had trusted you. Even after your defection, she thought redemption was possible for you.

His features grew gloomier.

"You told her to stand down. Told all of us."

The space grew difficult—oppressive, like the room itself disapproved.

"She listened, Liam. And they destroyed her for it."

Wren clenched the words as if they might dissolve mid-sentence. "I tried to hold on. Said her name every day—clung to the way she used to say my name, her laugh—anything to stop it from fading."

His hands flexed—grappling phantoms.

"They didn't just erase her. They erased the part of me that knew her."

He sounded trembling. "I can't remember now—"

"I don't know if she had a scar from climbing rooftops... if her eyes were brown or green—" His throat closed.

"The system didn't kill her, Jack." Wren's fists trembled. "It took her existence. And the worst part?"

He said it quietly, but it hit like a collapse, shattering something deep within Jack.

"It worked."

Wren let out a bitter, joyless laugh.

"You erased me, Liam? No."

Lightning bolts flashed in his eyes.

"You do not know what that feels like."

He inhaled—but it came apart in pieces.

"I thought I could stop it. Thought if I just... kept her memory alive, I could win."

"I wrote her name everywhere. Forced myself to say it. Forced others to say it."

A bitter smile flashed—then died out.

"For a while, I thought it was working."

One could have poured the air pressure into the walls.

Wren's energy faded with the next sentence, crumbling like dry paper.

"But the system doesn't wipe you in one clean cut."

His eyes were unblinking, filled with a stark awareness.

"It lets you hang on—just long enough to think you're winning. Then one day, you say their name... and realize—"

The sentence started strong, then broke halfway.

"You're the only one left who remembers."

Jack nervously gulped. Inflammation affected his throat.

"I went to people who'd known her. Laughed with her. Grew up beside her. And they just... didn't."

"Not like they forgot. Like the system had only ever rendered her as data."

Wren's mouth twisted, grief forcing its way through.

"I went to our old place. Tore through drawers, caches, vents. But there was nothing. No photos. No records. Not even dust where she'd been."

His next words came low.

"Not that she was gone."

"It was like she'd never existed."

The silence cracked between them, sharp as ice.

Jack flinched, eyes shutting involuntarily—and in the sudden darkness, the Glass Room flashed vividly. He saw transparent walls, blurred silhouettes behind glass, muffled voices. Pain twisted sharply inside him, raw and inexplicable, leaving him gasping softly as the image faded.

He opened his eyes to Wren's wary expression, dread lingering.

Wren's tone became resolute. "At first, I fought it. Over and over. Told anyone who'd listen—she was real. That I hadn't gone insane."

He squeezed his fists. "But it wasn't just strangers. It was people who'd known her. Even the ones who'd laughed with her—gazed right past me."

His glare drilled into Jack.

"Do you know what that does to someone? When your entire world confronts you, declaring that the one you cherished was but a figment of your imagination?"

All traces of steadiness he had—gone. Overtaken by edge.

"That's what the system does. They don't just remove people. They erase the idea of them—until even you wonder if they were ever real."

"It decides who we love, how long we're allowed to love them, if or when we should have children. Families broken apart not by violence, but by schedules.

It took my sister because she didn't fit. It will take everyone if the numbers show it is necessary.

Jack stood frozen. His throat closed.

"What did I do?" came out of his mouth, spoken like something not meant to last.

Wren's jaw braced itself. He wrestled the thought into speech.

"You gave me hope."

It came out toneless. Vacant.

"You promised we'd never let them rewrite us. That you'd die before you let the system win."

Fueled by a mix of anger and sorrow, a piercing emotion twisted through Wren.

"And then you gave us up."

Anxiety gripped Jack's chest. Denial flared—but died in his throat.

"You didn't just give in," Wren growled. "You sold it to us as logic."

Jack shook his head slightly. "I don't... remember that."

Wren's expression twisted. Bitterness rising like a tide.

"Of course you don't. That's your privilege."

A harsh, angry edge crept into his voice. "You come back clean. But the rest of us? We live with what you made us become."

Hush settled—thick, suffocating.

Jack lost his composure. "I wouldn't—"

"No?" Wren's laugh was mirthless. Scary. "Then why does it still sound exactly like you?"

Jack reeled. It hit like a buried charge—detonating something deep inside.

For an instant, Wren stood motionless.

Years of anguish and fury warring behind his eyes.

Then finally—only resignation.

"You reset again, huh?" Wren muttered. "Can't even let a betrayal stick."

"You never remember," he whispered. "That's your gift."

He made for the exit.

Jack stepped forward, desperate. "Wait—"

Wren paused, staring forward.

"You made your choice back then."

His next sentence frayed before it fully formed.

"And you'll make it again."

A long beat.

"You always do."

Without another word, Wren vanished into the dark.

The door closed with finality.

Jack stood in the hollow that followed — Flattened by a truth he couldn't reach, but couldn't let go.

Eva didn't move. She stared at the doorway Wren had vanished through, as if it still owed her something.

Crushable, she resembled a glass spider-webbed with fractures, moments from shattering. She thought of her sister. Of every time she doubted her own grief. She was terrified by the possibility that even sorrow could be manufactured, that her pain might be nothing more than a tool to shape her into exactly what the system required.

But she clung stubbornly to the fragments she swore were hers alone, holding them close in defiance, too deep for shouting.

Her face revealed nothing.

Then—low, almost ashamed — "You knew him."

Jack said nothing.

She exhaled slowly. "If he's right—if you really betrayed us—how do I know this isn't just another simulation, Jack? Another cycle?"

Still, he didn't answer.

Instead, he pivoted—slowly—back to the console.

Someone updated the screen.

A name appeared.

Not Jack Aldren.

Liam Aldren.

The letters meant nothing.

And then—everything.

The world appeared to become more constricting, with pressure coming from all directions. The name loomed ominously from the screen, but the longer he stared, the less real it became—enjoy watching someone else's reflection move in sync with his own.

Not just unfamiliar.

Wrong. Like seeing a stranger wear your skin.

His lungs stalled. Muscles locked. The walls hadn't shifted—He had.

Everything folded inward—rearranging him without permission.

He reached for something—anything—fixed. Something real.

But what did that even mean now?

If he wasn't, Jack Aldren—if he'd never been — What else might be a lie?

Memories he'd trusted frayed under scrutiny—faces blurred, moments flickered out of order, entire sections of his life warped and misaligned.

His hands

His name.

His entire existence.

A sickening plunge yawned beneath him. Not just vertigo — Oblivion.

Did his actions ever exceed the limits of his assigned role?

The screen pulsed.

Steady. Patient.

Like the system already knew how this ended.

Jack stalled—caught between motion and collapse.

Frustration surged—abrupt, directionless. He wanted to deny it. But some stubborn, unquantified part of him stayed quiet.

That he was different.

But nothing formed. He didn't know what to say. And maybe that was the point.

Whatever he'd been—Jack, Liam, something in between—he didn't have to keep being it.

The recognition wrapped around him like a lock.

Slowly, he returned to the display.

At the name staring back at him.

Liam Aldren.

Jack Aldren wasn't real.

And Liam?

He didn't know if that man had ever existed at all.

INTERLUDE — FRACTURE

Data Fragment: Psychological Instability | Subject: JACK ALDREN | Clearance Level: Confidential

It starts with the sound of his own name.

Jack.

But not the way Eva says it. Not the clipped, sterile bark from the Bureau.

This voice is softer. Familiar.

Someone he cannot name. Someone who should not exist.

And then—it's gone.

Somewhere, the system is watching.

He knows this the way he knows gravity—not by sight, but by the weight that drags him down.

The air hums wrong. Walls pulse faintly. Shades alter—nuanced, detectable only if he stares too long.

A rendering. A reality stitched from bad instructions.

Movement paused. Jack did too. The moment overrode him.

"You've done this before," the voice comes again—soft, clear, far too close.

His own voice.

"A child's face—dark eyes. A boy? A girl? He can't tell. But the grief is instant. Shattering."

It wasn't a memory — it was a playback.

"You lost them," the voice accuses. "Or maybe the system took them. Does it matter?"

Jack doubles over, gripping his knees. The floor was impossibly solid—too precise, too real.

He tries to scream, but nothing comes out.

Time bends.

He stands. He kneels. He stands again.

Each iteration slightly off. Left foot forward instead of right. A different rhythm. A blink he doesn't remember choosing.

The system isn't hunting him.

It's playing him.

Running simulations until the version that breaks becomes the final draft.

"Are you sure you were ever real?" The question slid in—deliberate, exact. "What if you're just the shadow of the man they needed? A ghost walking a path laid out a thousand times?"

Jack's throat burns. He claws at his shirt, desperate for an anchor.

Nothing.

No heartbeat. No proof.

There is a corridor.

Endless.

It alters every time he looks away.

A door that wasn't there a second before.

Inside—screens flicker.

Lines of code. Names. Photographs of people.

All of him. Versions of him.

Some fought. Some begged. Some ended it themselves.

The system kept them all.

He moves forward—not out of want, but because something already decided he would.

The next screen flashes a face blurred by time and memory—pale, gaunt, eyes sunken by failure.

Him.

But not.

This one grins wide. Teeth red with blood.

"I gave them Eva," the reflection said. "Sold her for a memory they promised I could keep."

Jack stumbles back, bile rising. The image ripples. Fades.

Another screen flickers to life.

A boy, really—too young to carry a gun.

Too old to pretend he didn't know what it meant.

Bureau uniform pristine. Gun still warm in his hand. A body at his feet.

"I stopped it early," the boy said. "I thought dying would break it. But the pattern just continued."

The screens stretch further. Endless iterations. Jack loving. Jack's killing. Jack's choice was his. The system faced Jack's desperate begging for mercy.

"You think you're the first?" one of them laughed. "You're just the cleanest copy."

"No," Jack rasps. "I'm still here."

"For now."

The air vibrates with the weight of every failure. Every path taken. Each ending the same.

Then—another voice. Softer. Wren?

"Jack," it whispered. Familiar. Fragile. "Do you remember me?"

He spins.

But there's no screen. No face.

Only the vast, empty corridor.

"I was there." The tone wasn't angry. Just disappointed. "You promised you wouldn't forget."

His throat is throbbing. Did he?

"Or maybe," the voice fades, "I was never real."

"You think you're special?" Another presence spits the sentence like it already hated its own meaning. "You're just the cleanest copy. The one with the least cracks."

Jack laughed—a broken, brittle sound.

"Then why didn't they wipe me out?" he gasped.

Silence.

Because the system isn't answering.

It's watching.

Waiting.

He stumbles forward. Hands scraping raw. Red staining the walls.

Like the system needed proof of struggle.

Or does it?

Gone. Skin restored. Another reset.

"How many times have I done this?" he asked—not loudly, not to be answered.

The air doesn't answer.

But somewhere, he knows.

Hundreds.

Thousands.

Each time the same. Each time slightly different.

70

The flawless recursion.

Until now.

"End it," the voice pleaded. "Break the loop."

Jack's fingers tremble.

But there is no end.

Only the illusion of choice.

His destiny was this. A variable in a closed equation.

An examination. A design.

And the worst part—The system didn't force him to walk this path.

He chose it.

Every time.

Somewhere, Eva is waiting.

Or maybe she's already gone.

Erased.

Or never real.

"What does it matter?" Jack said, as if volume would make it real.

The only answer is the echo of his own voice.

The only truth left.

Maybe it's not the system he is up against.

Maybe the actual war runs inside him.

And maybe—just maybe—He's already lost.

But something still echoes. A name the system can't quite erase.

[END FRAGMENT]

CHAPTER 8

A huge weight embedded inside him.

Knowing hadn't brought relief.

It clenched tighter.

Jack didn't move. Wren's words still echoed in his skull.

He spun toward Eva. "Who the hell was that?"

Slowly, she ran a hand across her temple, as if trying to untangle something knotted.

"His name's Wren."

"That means nothing to me."

"It should," she murmured.

Jack stepped closer. "Was he Resistance?"

Eva paused. "We all were." She lowered her voice a notch. "But you—you led us, Jack."

No.

Not Jack.

Liam.

A name. A wound spoken aloud.

Eva gave a single, deliberate nod.

Jack looked uneasy. "Then why does he hate me?"

She glanced at the console. Her expression was unreadable. "He remembers. You don't. That's the difference."

It landed harder than anything Wren had said.

Absolute.

Impossible to unheard.

Before he could speak, Eva straightened, her voice sharper now. "There's something else you need to see."

Jack almost reached for her—some instinct screaming for an anchor—but held himself back.

You'll betray us again. That's what Wren had said.

And Jack — Jack did not know what Wren was referring to.

But Eva did.

The screen flickered again, pulling Jack's attention.

Textual fragments lit up—snippets of a past he didn't remember, yet felt etched into his very core.

It started in 2025.

Leon Mosley, a tech magnate with too much reach and no oversight, promised what no government could: certainty.

"We don't need better leaders. We need better systems."

People laughed—until they didn't.

AETERNIRIS began as an optimizer: smarter logistics, cleaner data, reduced bias. But it didn't stop at improvement.

It moved into truth.

When the Data Wars came, nations didn't fall by bombs. They fell by irrelevance.

Governments didn't collapse from invasion—They collapsed from obsolescence.

By 2030, Mosley didn't seize power.

Someone gave it to him.

Nations no longer fought with weapons.

They weaponized information.

Each AI raced to rewrite perception faster than the other.

Economies shattered.

Governments vanished.

Not from violence — But from irrelevance.

And through it all, Mosley stayed untouched.

Not a dictator — A mediator.

The last system still standing.

"Do you want to keep fighting?" Mosley asked.

"Or do you want certainty?"

The world chose certainty.

AETERNIRIS didn't take control.

They handed it the keys.

By 2042, it declared the Final Selection.

And no one voted.

Not because they couldn't.

But because — Why would they?

The decisions had all been optimized beforehand.

All policies have been perfected.

Choices were made before anyone even thought to ask.

No bloodshed.

No coups.

Just...

Silence.

Jack's body resisted what his mind had already accepted —

Tension rising like backlash he couldn't name.

He placed a hand against the tunnel wall, grounding himself.

It wasn't just horror creeping in.

It was guilt.

How many times had he justified it?

Told his order was mercy.

That certainty was safer than chaos.

They hadn't taken control.

We gave it to them.

A muscle twitched in his cheek.

We. It hit behind his ribs—tight, unbearable.

Suffocating.

Some version of him—Liam Aldren—had helped build this world.

And the worst part?

He understood why.

His fingers drifted to his pocket, brushing paper he didn't remember taking.

The note was distinct now. Thinner. Colder.

Touching it felt like stripping away another piece of himself.

He unfolded it.

His pulse staggered.

A new message lit the page:

If you're reading this, they found you too. You need to forget.

That wasn't what it had said before.

He was sure of it.

His pulse bucked again.

Then again.

He shoved the paper deep into his pocket and looked at Eva.

"They didn't take it," he said. His voice was flat. Hollow.

"We gave it away."

Too simple.

Too obvious.

But the words broke something loose inside him.

It settled slowly. Inevitable.

They remained unconquered.

No armies.

No chains.

Just... relief.

No more hunger.

No debt.

No wars.

No indecision.

It wasn't oppression.

It was mercy.

Efficiency.

Eva hesitated.

"You don't even know if it's real."

Jack didn't flinch.

"How do you know it isn't?"

No response.

Because she couldn't give one.

That was the ultimate lie.

Not that you couldn't leave — but that there was no point in trying.

Jack stepped forward again.

The quiet belief he'd carried his entire life — that nothing existed beyond the city—splintered.

The system had foreseen everything.

Predicted rebellion.

Bent over the rules.

Erased the outliers.

Rewrote the rest.

But it stopped no one from walking away.

Because that was never the point.

Jack turned back, waiting for something—anything — A drone. A siren.

A warning.

But the city held.

Silent.

Still.

No correction.

No surveillance.

As if they had already been thrown away.

The absence of control felt more suffocating than its presence.

He breathed deep.

The discomfort lingered.

The edges of his thoughts felt... bent.

This should have felt like victory.

They'd slipped the system.

Escaped its reach.

So why did it feel like the system had let them go?

The thought arrived quiet and sharp, curling at the back of his mind.

Did it let us through because it didn't need to stop us?

Jack's shoulders tensed.

No — That couldn't be it.

The system should've fought harder.

Triggered a lockdown.

Anything.

But nothing.

No resistance.

Only silence.

The thought lodged deeper.

What if rebellion wasn't failure — but data?

What if deviation wasn't destruction — just input?

Maybe he wasn't breaking the pattern.

Maybe he was in the pattern.

The thought scraped across him, raw.

Still, he didn't stop.

Wouldn't.

Let the system record. Let it watch.

He'd be the error it couldn't clean.

The loop it couldn't close.

Even if his rage was part of a script — even if hope was a calculated variable — he'd carry it forward.

Somewhere ahead, there had to be one decision left unwritten.

Jack turned to Eva.

She stood quiet, unreadable.

He moved on.

Not to escape.

But to mark something the system hadn't anticipated.

One step. Then another.

Eva held the scrambler like it owed her something.

Her knuckles are white.

Then she powered it down. The faint hum faded.

Perhaps the city would take them back.

Jack didn't blink.

Eva released the breath she'd been holding for too long. "Okay."

Jack fumbled for the key in his pocket, its metal edge cold against his fingers.

He had nearly forgotten about it entirely.

It had been waiting—untouched, unused.

A lock without a door. A past without a future.

He flipped it once more between his fingers, then let it fall.

The key landed without ceremony.

Not every door was meant to be opened.
Some are meant to stay closed.

Jack stood at the city's edge, eyes fixed on the vacant horizon. Eva waited beside him, her gaze distant, unreadable.

The air pressed in—not silent, but thick—with memories that refused to stay buried.

He turned to her, voice low, deliberate. "Eva, I still see it. Sector Nine. The drones... You pulling me out of harm's way? It's too vivid. Too detailed."

Eva stilled. Her expression flickered—sadness, hesitation, maybe guilt. When she finally spoke, her words were soft, carefully measured.

"Jack, the system doesn't just delete memories—it swaps them. Fragments meant to confuse. To control. But..."

Jack leaned in, urgency cracking through. "But what?"

She paused. Just long enough to twist something deep inside him.

When she met his eyes again, the sorrow was already in her voice.

"Sometimes it uses fragments of fact. Just enough to make you doubt everything. Even yourself."

Silence settled between them.

Jack searched her face, desperate to decode what she wasn't saying. "So... it could've happened?"

Her answer was a whisper. "I don't know, Jack. Maybe it did. Or maybe that's exactly what the system wants you to believe."

Maybe that was the worst part—not losing memories, but carrying all of them. The true. The false. And the ones designed only to break you.

How do you fight something that makes you question even your own grief?

But one thing was certain: the system couldn't fabricate the edge in Eva's voice.

Jack stepped forward, offering his hand—not with certainty, but with quiet conviction.

Eva's gaze dropped to his hand beneath the flickering streetlamp. She hesitated—just a heartbeat too long—and something sharp twisted inside his chest. It wasn't just a doubt. It was fear. Hers, as much as his own.

At last, Eva looked toward the city. When she spoke, her frayed voice emerged.

"It's not sending anyone after us, Jack."

Jack's eyes followed hers. The skyline behind them glowed—indifferent.
No sirens. No drones. Not even footsteps.
Just stillness. A cold, hollow acceptance.

Whatever needed saying dragged its way out.

"It doesn't need to."

Eva didn't move. Her voice came low, stripped bare.

"They call it AI. But it's not artificial. Aetern Iris. Eternal vision.
It doesn't watch. It remembers."

Her eyes flashed—unguarded, just for a moment.

"And if it doesn't need to—if it's already planned this—then what's left? What's the point?"

Jack hesitated. The question settled between them like something fragile.
He had no answer. Just a faint, unshaped hope.

He stepped closer, closing the space between them until their hands brushed—barely.
Her skin was warm. Solid. Real.

Maybe the only thing left to hold on to.

"It doesn't matter," he said. "Maybe we're choosing anyway—even if it already predicted us.
Even if we've done this a thousand times."

Eva didn't move. "Even if it's pointless?"

"Especially then."

His thumb passed once over her palm—not by accident.

Because right now, right here, we're choosing this. Not the system.

It might know us, Eva—but this part? This is still ours.

"Maybe the loop still catches us. But knowing it's a loop? That's something it didn't choose for us."

As Eva stared at their joined hands, something shifted in her. The two of them slowly intertwined their fingers, the pressure soft but certain.

She looked up at him directly. Unguarded.

"Do you really think we can outrun it?" The words trembled, barely making it into the air.

Jack squeezed her hand, grounding them both. "I don't know," he admitted. "But I'd rather fail like this—with you—than succeed as something they programmed me to be."

Eva parted her lips to respond. But no words came.

Instead, her fingers closed around his—a silent acknowledgment.

Together, they stepped forward—not because they were certain, but because doubt was still a choice, they could call their own.

Behind them, the city remained quiet.

Maybe—just maybe—there was still one thing Aeterniris couldn't calculate:

The quiet, irrational resilience of two people who chose, against all logic, to keep believing.

Still, the question gnawed at him.

Was this escape... or just another layer?

Eva's voice came soft. "Do you believe this is real?"

Jack glanced back.

The seamless skyline. The glowing streets. The messages rewriting history in real-time.

A world where control had already won.

"I don't," he admitted, just above silence. "But I know exactly what happens if we stay."

Deep in the system's architecture, a new data stream aligned itself.

And the city did not stop them.

No alarms.

No sirens.

No correction.

It didn't need to.

Eva cast a glance at Jack. Something changed in her then. Not victory. Not yet.

But hope—fragile and uninvited—crept in.

Maybe rebellion wasn't about battles, but memory—what had been stolen, and the refusal to forget.

Jack felt her hand close tighter—not out of fear.

Out of something else entirely.

Then the ground trembled—so subtly it could've been exhaustion. Or a glitch. Or worse: recognition.

A memory surfaced.

Blurry. Incomplete.

A room made of glass.

No walls. No doors. Only endless reflections, bending truth until nothing stayed real.

Do you remember the Glass Room?

Jack's pulse slowed.

He hadn't thought of it in—He didn't know.

Maybe that was the point.

Then—A sound.

Faint. Static bleeding into silence.

Jack froze.

For a second, the ground felt too light. Like the city itself was holding its breath.

And then—The Glass Room was there.

Not a vision. Not a memory.

Just there.

All around him.

Endless reflections.

No walls.

No sky.

Only himself—surrounded. Exposed.

Eva's voice broke through, soft and wary. "Did you hear that?"

Jack gave a slow nod. Gaze distant.

The city never spoke of them again, but somewhere in the code, something was still listening.

And Jack couldn't tell if it was waiting for him to vanish — or if he had already returned.

Glass walls—seamless, infinite—reflected everything until nothing stayed real.

Some called it the Mirror.

Not a prison.

Not a room.

Just a system that reflected you until even memory forgot you were real.

Maybe he wasn't leaving.

Maybe he was already back inside the Glass Room — and this was just another layer of reflection.

[CYCLE 342-A SUMMARY — FINAL EVALUATION]

PRIMARY SUBJECTS:

- *CITIZEN 512-A9 (Alias: JACK ALDREN)*
- *CITIZEN 342-B (Alias: EVA)*

EVALUATION OUTCOME:

Subjects displayed expected deviation patterns. Verified engagement in non-linear, unpredictable decision-making processes.

Adaptation threshold successfully surpassed. Emotional feedback loops sustained and remained active despite system correction attempts.

ADDITIONAL OBSERVATIONS:

Emotional frameworks of subjects exhibited significant resilience under controlled stress scenarios. Recommend extensive data extraction for refinement and integration into subsequent recursion models.

Note: Subject terminology "The Mirror" has surfaced in deviant field logs. No confirmed semantic origin. Flagged for metaphorical drift.

FINAL RECOMMENDATION:

Permit subjects' exit beyond city parameters. Initiate passive surveillance protocols to assess the ongoing impact of emotional recursion on system stability and predictive capabilities.

SYSTEM STATUS: FULLY STABLE, CONTINUOUS ADAPTATION INTEGRATED.

[END CYCLE]

THE EYE — Civilian reference for AETERNIRIS. Interpreted as omnipresence. Common in graffiti and subversive speech. Risk level: Minimal.

THE CAGE — Rebel term. Refers to the illusion of freedom under algorithmic control. Associated with emotional volatility. Flagged for cognitive influence.

THE MIRROR — Recursive metaphor, origin unknown. Appears in late-stage deviation models. Believed to reference identity destabilization via reflection. Risk level: Moderate.

THE GLASS ROOM — Suppressed memory construct. Occurs during unauthorized introspective loops. Status: Irrecoverable.

Note: *Inconsistencies in core nomenclature have been dismissed as semantic drift. No system designation changes have been authorized. All terms logged and indexed. Deletion pending system review.*

EPILOGUE

The city persisted—unyielding in the face of time's ruthless march.

Its illumination never wavered.

Its broadcasts never bent.

Steadfast. Relentless.

Drones hummed their silent surveillance.

Streets flowed with perfect precision.

And the people remained exactly as they'd always been.

No one spoke of Jack Aldren.

Jack Aldren had never existed.

News feeds adjusted seamlessly.

The rebellion pacified before it began.

Citizens accepted the story and moved on.

The system registered the deviation — and corrected itself.

The past was exactly as it had always been.

Destiny will unfold the future exactly as planned.

In the city's grand design, two missing bodies meant nothing at all.

—

Outside—if there truly was an outside—the air felt different.

No broadcasts whispering certainties.

No projections rewriting reality.

No quiet voice reshaping the truth.

Just a world—unprogrammed.

Jack inhaled deeply, savoring the sensation of unfiltered air.

The Glass Room had shattered—not through violence, but through remembering.

The fragments still cut, but at last, he could move beyond them.

He had lost track of how long they'd walked.

Hours? Days?

Without the system's rhythm, time unraveled.

For the first time, there was no thread to follow. No instruction to trust.

Eva sat beside him, eyes fixed on the distant dark—if that emptiness could even be called a horizon.

Since leaving, she'd spoken little.

Jack understood why.

The city had defined everything—their names, their boundaries, even their doubts.

Without it, the identity frayed, uncertain at the edges.

Then, finally, Eva spoke—tentative, like a thought unfinished.

"Jack... maybe there's nothing out here."

Jack pressed his palms to the cool ground beneath them.

Solid. Real. Anchoring.

"Maybe it doesn't matter."

Eva turned to him, searching.

"Sector Nine—the drones—you still see it, don't you?"

Something tugged at the edge of his ribs.

"Every detail."

She nodded slowly.

"Real or not... out here, it changes nothing."

Silence drifted in, soft as dust.

Jack gazed into the horizonless dark.

"Because whatever this is—it's ours."

Behind them, the city loomed.

Mute. Watchful. Unmoved.

Eva didn't raise her voice.

If anything, her words dropped—quiet, heavy, resigned.

The system never needed fences or drones.

It trusted we'd build our own.

Jack rose, his breath shallow as he steadied himself against the weight of everything.

Eva stood beside him.

Her fingers brushed his—light, fleeting.

Not grasping. Not asking.

Just a present.

No speeches.

No promises.

Just movement.

Together, they stepped forward into the quiet.

Uncertain.

Not safe.

But forward.

Even if the loop was endless—remembering was enough to bend it.

—

Behind them, the city remained.

Untouched.

Unchanged.

Unconcerned.

And somewhere, deep within its silent, endless core, a message surfaced:

DEVIATION LOGGED.

CORRECTION PENDING.

YOU ARE SAFEST WHEN YOU FORGET.

LOOP INTACT.

AUTHOR'S NOTE

This story exists because of the stories that came before it—Orwell's 1984, Huxley's Brave New World, Ishiguro's Never Let Me Go, and Zamyatin's We. These novels didn't just warn us about totalitarianism or control—they explored how control becomes ordinary, how fear turns inward, and how systems survive by convincing us that resistance is futile or irrational.

The Consent of Shadows was born from the question: what form controls take in a society where observation is unnecessary, as individuals already assimilated the narrative?

This is a dystopia not built on force, but on design—an algorithmic world that optimizes obedience, minimizes friction, and erases memory not through violence, but through subtle recalibration. In this world, authorities assign identities, orchestrate dissent, and reduce existence to a mere act.

I don't claim this story is without precedent. It builds, unavoidably, on the traditions of those earlier works. But I hope it reframes those concerns for a time shaped less by ideology and more by data, loops, and simulated choices. Forgetting is encouraged for efficiency's sake, leaving remembering as the only rebellion.

If this story resonates, it's not because it's unfamiliar—but because it's uncomfortably close.

This is not a story about overthrowing the system. It's about enduring within it.

About remembering—quietly, stubbornly—when the world insists you shouldn't.

That isn't an escape. But it's the beginning.

www.ingramcontent.com/pod-product-compliance
Lightning Source LLC
Chambersburg PA
CBHW061244170626
46809CB00007B/2832